Dedicated To:
All the children in the
world who love dogs.

That Dog named Sherry
Written by
Priscilla Dawn Baer

Once upon a day there was a dog named Sherry.

She had pink fur and nose like a berry.

She would run from anything scary.

She had a bone she liked to bury.

Her dinner was mostly dairy.

She had a friend named Larry.

The mail she liked to carry.

This ball she gave to Cherry.

Meet Mary, Jerry, and Terry.

This week they are her fairies.

That saved her on the prairy.

From a leapord that was hairy.

The End!

For this book you paid Denarii for my Ferrari.

About the Author:

Priscilla Loves Dogs!

Priscilla is the Author of :
What Happens in a Flower Patch
The Lonely Umbrella
Saul the Salamander

www.ingramcontent.com/pod-product-compliance
Lightning Source LLC
Chambersburg PA
CBHW041006170626
46815CB00002B/184